TABLE OF CONTENTS

PUBLISHED BY AXPONE PRESS

INTRODUCTION - WHAT ARE AXOLOTLS? "(AK-SUH-LO-TL)".

AXOLOTLS, SCIENTIFICALLY KNOWN AS AMBYSTOMA MEXICANUM, ARE A GROUP OF INCREDIBLY UNIQUE AMPHIBIANS THAT COME FROM THE MURKY FRESHWATER LAKES AND CANALS OF XOCHIMILCO, NEAR MEXICO CITY.

IF YOU VISIT THERE, YOU CAN TAKE ONE OF THESE COLORFUL CRUISE BOATS DOWN THE RIVER!

THESE FASCINATING CREATURES ARE A TYPE OF MOLE SALAMANDER, CLOSELY RELATED TO TIGER SALAMANDERS. HOWEVER, AXOLOTLS ARE DISTINGUISHED BY THEIR UNBELIEVABLE ABILITY TO RETAIN JUVENILE FEATURES THROUGHOUT THEIR WHOLE LIFE, A PHENOMENON KNOWN AS NEOTENY.

UNLIKE MOST AMPHIBIANS, WHICH UNDERGO METAMORPHOSIS FROM LARVAL TO ADULT STAGES, AXOLOTLS REMAIN AQUATIC AND GILLED. THIS MEANS THEY BREATHE UNDERWATER THROUGH THEIR FEATHERY EXTERNAL GILLS, WHICH PROTRUDE FROM BEHIND THEIR HEADS. THIS TRAIT HAS MADE THEM A SUBJECT OF INTRIGUE AND EXTENSIVE STUDY BY MANY SCIENTISTS AROUND THE WORLD.

AXOLOTLS POSSESS AN EXTRAORDINARY CAPACITY FOR REGENERATION, UNPARALLELED IN THE ANIMAL KINGDOM. THEY CAN REGENERATE NOT ONLY LIMBS BUT ALSO OTHER PARTS OF THEIR BODY, INCLUDING THEIR SPINAL CORD, HEART, AND PARTS OF THEIR BRAIN, WITHOUT SCARRING.

THIS REMARKABLE ABILITY OFFERS INVALUABLE INSIGHTS INTO REGENERATIVE HEALING PROCESSES AND THE POTENTIAL FOR APPLICATIONS IN HUMAN MEDICINE. RESEARCHERS HOPE THAT BY UNDERSTANDING HOW AXOLOTLS REGENERATE TISSUE, THEY MIGHT ONE DAY DEVELOP WAYS TO STIMULATE SIMILAR REGENERATIVE HEALING IN HUMANS!

DESPITE THEIR ALMOST MYTHICAL STATUS, AXOLOTLS ARE CRITICALLY ENDANGERED IN THE WILD. THEIR NATURAL HABITAT IN THE LAKES AND WATERWAYS OF XOCHIMILCO IS UNDER SEVERE THREAT.

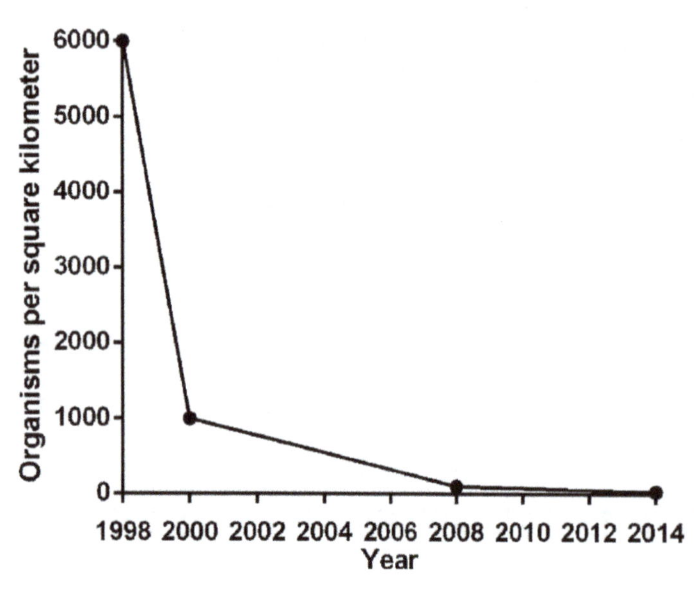

THIS IS DUE TO URBANIZATION, POLLUTION, AND THE INTRODUCTION OF INVASIVE SPECIES. CONSERVATION EFFORTS ARE IN PLACE TO PROTECT THESE UNIQUE ANIMALS, BUT THEIR WILD POPULATIONS CONTINUE TO DECLINE, AS SEEN ON THIS GRAPH.

WHAT MAKES THEM DIFFERENT TO TYPICAL SALAMANDERS?

ONE OF THE MAIN DIFFERENCES IS THAT AXOLOTLS (WE'LL CALL THEM AXIES FOR SHORT) ARE NEOTENIC - WHICH MEANS THAT THEY REMAIN AQUATIC AND RETAIN THEIR GILLS. THEREFORE. THEY DON'T UNDERGO METAMORPHOSIS OR DEVELOP LUNGS THAT WOULD HELP THEM WITH LIFE ON LAND. THEY ALSO HAVE REGENERATIVE ABILITIES, AND MANY OTHER COOL DIFFERENCES, WHICH WE'LL TALK ABOUT IN LATER PAGES OF THIS BOOK!

HOW DID THEY BECOME SO POPULAR?

AXIES - ROSE TO POPULARITY IN JUNE OF 2021, WHEN MINECRAFT FIRST INCLUDED THEM IN THE LATEST GAME UPDATE. THIS SPARKED A HUGE INTEREST IN THIS AMAZING ANIMAL.

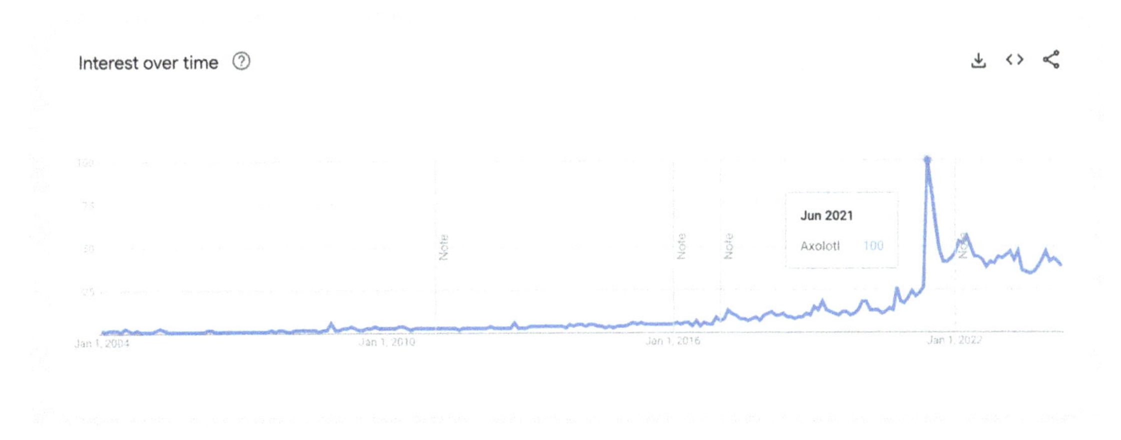

WHAT ARE SOME MYTHS ABOUT AXOLOTLS?

AXOLOTLS ARE FISH

EVEN THOUGH AXOLOTLS ARE COMMONLY REFERRED TO AS MEXICAN WALKING FISH, THEY ARE NOT ACTUALLY CLASSIFIED AS FISH BUT AS AMPHIBIANS!

AXOLOTLS PREFER WARM WATER

THIS SPECIES CAME FROM A LAKE WITH AN AVERAGE TEMPERATURE OF 17-18°C, SO IT IS ADVISABLE TO PREPARE A COOL AND FRESH WATER TO AVOID ANY SERIOUS PROBLEM DEVELOPING.

AXOLOTL IS THE AZTEC GOD OF FIRE AND LIGHTNING

ALTHOUGH IT IS AWESOME TO THINK THAT THIS TINY AND ADORABLE CREATURE HOLDS SUCH POWER, THERE'S NOT REALLY ANY EVIDENCE TO PROVE THIS. BUT HEY, WITH THEIR AMAZING REGENERATIVE ABILITY, THEY CAN STAY YOUNG FOR A VERY LONG TIME. HOW COOL IS THAT!

GRAVELS ARE SAFE TO USE IN AXOLOTL AQUARIUMS

DEPENDING ON THE GRAVEL THAT YOU WILL USE AS AXOLOTLS MIGHT INGEST THESE GRAVELS ACCIDENTALLY, AND BIG GRAVELS MIGHT CAUSE A SERIOUS PROBLEM LATER ON.

FROZEN BLOODWORMS ARE A GOOD SOURCE OF VITAMINS FOR AXOLOTLS

BLOODWORMS ARE NOT AT ALL NUTRITIOUS FOR AXOLOTLS. THEY ARE FATTY AND LOW IN PROTEIN. FEEDING YOUR PET BLOODWORMS OVER A LONG PERIOD OF TIME MIGHT CAUSE COMPLICATIONS IN THEIR HEALTH.

USING ANTIBIOTICS FOR AXOLOTL IS OKAY

USING ANY ANTIBIOTIC (EVEN BY MICRODOSING IT) IS DANGEROUS FOR YOUR PET. YOU SHOULD FIRST CONFIRM WHAT KIND OF BACTERIA YOU ARE DEALING WITH AND ASK THE VET FOR HELP.

GOLDFISH ARE GREAT TANKMATES FOR AXOLOTLS

IT IS NOT ADVISABLE TO PUT BOTH GOLDFISH AND AXOLOTL IN THE SAME TANK. ALTHOUGH AXOLOTLS ARE NOT GOOD HUNTERS, THEY WILL EAT ANYTHING THAT FITS IN THEIR MOUTH (FISH INCLUDED!) AND THERE ARE INSTANCES WHERE GOLDFISH MIGHT NIP AXOLOTL'S GILLS.

AXOLOTL BIOLOGY & LIFECYCLE

AN AXOLOTL IS A TYPE OF AMPHIBIAN THAT CAN LIVE FOR UP TO 10 TO 15 YEARS. THIS ADORABLE CREATURE CAN GROW UP TO 12 INCHES IN LENGTH WITH AN AVERAGE WEIGHT OF 8 OUNCES. DID YOU KNOW THAT THE AXOLOTL'S AVERAGE SIZE IS COMPARED TO A TEACUP? HOW COOL IS THAT!

YOU CAN EASILY IDENTIFY AN AXOLOTL BY ITS GILLS, WHICH LOOK LIKE FEATHERS. WHAT MAKES THIS CREATURE IRRESISTIBLY LOVABLE IS ITS LIDLESS EYES, MATCHED WITH THE SHAPE OF ITS MOUTH, WHICH ALWAYS SEEMED TO HAVE A SMILE ON IT.

DID YOU KNOW THAT AXOLOTLS VARY IN COLOR? THEY RANGE FROM PINKISH TO BROWNISH-GREEN. WHITE AND PINK ARE THE MOST POPULAR COLOR VARIETIES FOR PET OWNERS.

DURING THE COLDER MONTHS, AXOLOTLS ENTER THE SPAWNING SEASON IN WHICH NEW EGGS ARE LAID UP BY THE MATURE FEMALE AXOLOTL. THESE EGGS, CALLED LARVAE, ARE NORMALLY ATTACHED TO PLANTS OR ROCK MATERIALS THAT SERVE AS THEIR PROTECTION AGAINST PREDATORS.

AXOLOTL LARVAE UNDERGO A GROWTH CALLED METAMORPHOSIS, IN WHICH THEIR LARVAL FEATURES SLOWLY CHANGE INTO THEIR ADULT FORM. HOWEVER, THEIR DISTINCTLY DIFFERENT TRAIT FROM OTHER AMPHIBIANS IS THAT AXOLOTLS RETAIN THEIR LARVAE FORM.

AFTER WAITING FOR TWO WEEKS, THE EGGS WILL HATCH. HOWEVER, WITHOUT ANY PARENTS TO TAKE CARE OF THEM, THE NEWLY HATCHED AXOLOTL LARVAE WILL LEARN TO FEND FOR THEMSELVES VERY EARLY.

AN AXOLOTL'S HABITAT & IT'S FRIENDS

AXOLOTLS ARE THE BEST TYPE OF PET FOR PEOPLE WITH VERY LIMITED SPACE. THEY ARE VERY CUTE TO WATCH EVEN THOUGH THEY ARE VERY LAZY IN NATURE. THEY COULD STAY STILL FOR HOURS, AND WHEN THEY MOVE, THEY ARE VERY SLOW.

DID YOU KNOW THAT THEY ARE LAZIER IN COLDER WATER CONDITIONS AND MORE ACTIVE IN WARMER WATER CONDITIONS? AXOLOTLS ARE KNOWN AS CARNIVORES, SO WHEN THEY ARE IN THEIR NATURAL ENVIRONMENT, AXOLOTLS ARE IDENTIFIED AS PREDATORS AND WILL EAT INSECTS, SMALL FISH, MOLLUSKS, AND WORMS.

THIS IS THE REASON WHY IT IS NOT ADVISABLE TO KEEP DIFFERENT-SIZED AXOLOTLS IN ONE AQUARIUM. CANNIBALISM CAN BE A PROBLEM WHEN THEY ARE KEPT TOGETHER AND NOT FED PROPERLY.

SHOULD YOU PLAN TO UPGRADE YOUR AXOLOTL TANK AND ADD A FEW TANK MATES, YOU SHOULD CAREFULLY CONSIDER THE SPECIES THAT YOU WILL ADD. CREATURES THAT MOSTLY KEPT TO THEMSELVES AND ENJOYED COLD WATER TEMPERATURES ARE THE BEST OPTIONS. YOU SHOULD TAKE NOTE OF THEIR SIZE AS YOUR AXOLOTLS MIGHT EAT THEM.

SOME OF THE PERFECT TANK MATES INCLUDE WHITE CLOUD MOUNTAIN MINNOWS. THESE ARE PEACEFUL CREATURES ALTHOUGH YOU HAVE TO KEEP IN MIND THAT YOUR AXOLOTL MIGHT EAT THEM. HOWEVER, THEY DON'T HAVE ANY SPINE, SO THEY ARE SAFE FOR YOUR AXOLOTLS TO EAT.

ZEBRA DANIOS ARE VERY AGILE FISH, SO THEY CAN EASILY ESCAPE THEIR PREDATOR. THEY MOSTLY STAY AWAY FROM YOUR AXOLOTL. HOWEVER, DO EXPECT THAT A FEW FISH WILL BE EATEN EVERY NOW AND THEN.

ANOTHER POSSIBLE TANK MATE IS GUPPIES. SOME OWNERS INTENTIONALLY PUT GUPPIES IN THE TANK AS SNACKS FOR AXOLOTL. GUPPIES REPRODUCE VERY FAST SO THE SUDDEN INCREASE OF THIS FISH IN THE TANK MIGHT STRESS YOUR AXOLOTL.

ADULT APPLE SNAILS ARE SAFE TO KEEP IN ONE AQUARIUM TOGETHER WITH A SMALL AXOLOTL. HOWEVER, JUST LIKE GUPPIES, APPLE SNAILS REPRODUCE AT HIGH SPEED.

FISH TO AVOID PUTTING IN THE SAME AQUARIUM

THERE ARE A LOT OF FISH SPECIES YOU SHOULD AVOID PUTTING IN THE SAME TANK AS YOUR AXOLOTL. ONE OF THEM IS GOLDFISH. MANY OWNERS THINK THAT GOLDFISH ARE A GREAT TANK MATE FOR AXOLOTLS. HOWEVER, GOLDFISH ARE KNOWN AS FIN-NIPPERS, AND THEY WOULD OFTEN BULLY AXOLOTLS.

ASIDE FROM GOLDFISH, OTHER TYPES OF FISH YOU SHOULD AVOID ARE THE CORY CATFISH, OTOCINCLUS CATFISH, AND SHRIMPS.

CORY CATFISH AND OTOCINCLUS CATFISH HAS SHARP SPINES THAT CAN INJURE YOUR AXOLOTLS IF THEY EAT THEM. WHILE SHRIMPS ARE NOT IDEAL TANK MATES UNLESS YOU WILL PUT THEM AS SNACKS FOR YOUR AXOLOTL.

DIET, FOOD & HUNTING METHOD

AXOLOTL'S HUNTING METHOD

AXOLOTLS BURROW IN THE MUD AND HIDE IN OTHER AQUATIC PLANTS DURING THE DAY TO AVOID PREDATORS. HOWEVER, THEY ARE MORE ACTIVE WHEN THE SUN'S DOWN AND THAT'S WHEN THEY HUNT. WHEN EATING THEIR PREY, AXOLOTLS USE A SUCTION METHOD WHEN FEEDING. THEY SUCK UP TINY ORGANISMS SUCH AS CRUSTACEANS, WORMS, AND SMALL FISHES.

THEY WOULD ALSO SUCK SOME GRAVEL FROM TIME TO TIME TO HELP GRIND UP THEIR FOOD FOR EASIER DIGESTION.

AXOLOTLS WILL ALSO EAT LIVE OR EVEN DEAD FOOD. USING THEIR SENSE OF SMELL, AXOLOTL CAN DETECT THEIR PREY. ASIDE FROM THEIR SENSE OF SMELL. AXOLOTLS CAN ALSO DETECT MOVEMENT FROM LIVE PREY. ONCE DETECTED, AXOLOTL WILL 'SNAP' AT ITS MEAL.

DID YOU KNOW THAT AXOLOTLS ARE CLASSIFIED AS CARNIVORES? IN THE WILD, THEIR DIET CONSISTS OF FISH, MOLLUSKS, WORMS, AND EVEN INSECTS. WHILE IN CAPTIVITY, THEIR DIET IS SIMILAR WHICH CONSISTS OF FEEDS LIKE TROUTS AND SALMON PELLETS, EARTHWORMS AND FISH FEEDERS.

FROZEN FOODS

FROZEN BRINE SHRIMPS

AXOLOTLS ALSO EAT FROZEN BRINE SHRIMP. THESE ARE HIGH IN NUTRIENTS, WHICH IS A GOOD FOOD SOURCE FOR AXOLOTL. YOU CAN EASILY BUY THEM IN SHOPS, AND YOU CAN STORE THEM IN THE FREEZER.

TILAPIA

FROZEN TILAPIA IS ALSO A HEALTHY STAPLE FOR YOUR AXOLOTL. HOWEVER, KEEP IN MIND THAT YOU SHOULD AVOID BUYING SALTWATER TILAPIA AS IT IS HIGH IN SALT CONCENTRATION AND OTHER MINERALS THAT ARE NOT GOOD FOR YOUR AXOLOTL.

LIVE FOODS

EARTHWORMS

EARTHWORMS ARE GREAT FOR AXOLOTLS. THEY CONTAIN VARIOUS NUTRIENTS SUCH AS PROTEIN AND OTHER BENEFICIAL FATS. YOU CAN ALSO FEED YOUR AXOLOTL FROZEN EARTHWORM. HOWEVER, YOU MUST AVOID BUYING EARTHWORMS RAISED IN THE SOIL AS THEY COULD CONTAIN PESTICIDES.

BABY BRINE SHRIMPS

THIS FOOD IS GREAT FOR NEWLY HATCHED AXOLOTLS AS AXOLOTL LARVAE WILL ONLY CONSUME MOVING PREY FOR THE FIRST FEW WEEKS AFTER HATCHING.

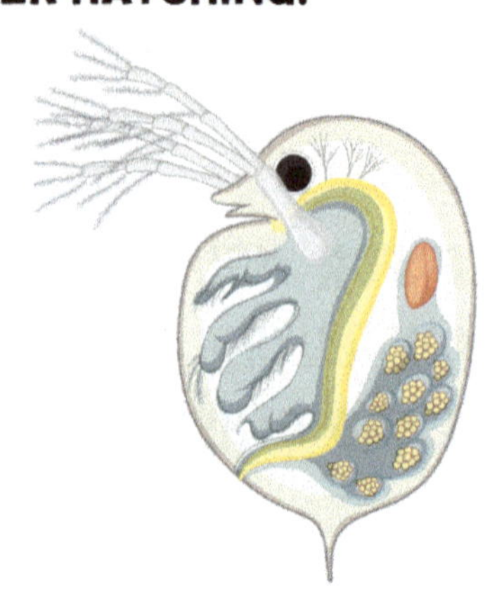

DAPHNIA

THIS IS A SMALL WATER CRUSTACEAN THAT IS PACKED WITH ESSENTIAL NUTRIENTS AND HEALTHY FATS. THIS FOOD IS ALSO PERFECT FOR NEWLY HATCHED AXOLOTL LARVAE.

BLACKWORM

BLACKWORM IS A GOOD SOURCE OF PROTEIN, PERFECT FOR NEWLY HATCHED AXOLOTL LARVAE. BLACKWORMS CAN CONSIDERED AS AN EASIER CULTURE THAT YOU CAN CREATE AND MAINTAIN.

PELLETS

THERE ARE A LOT OF FOOD PELLETS THAT YOU CAN CHOOSE FROM. THEY ALSO VARY IN NUTRITIONAL VALUES AND THE AMOUNT THAT YOU SHOULD FEED YOUR AXOLOTL.

HERE ARE SOME PELLET FOODS THAT YOU CAN GIVE YOUR PET.

- SALMON PELLETS
- HIKARI SINKING PELLETS
- SHRIMP PELLETS
- RANGEN AXOLOTL PELLETS

YOU HAVE TO MAKE SURE THAT THE PELLET FOODS THAT YOU WILL BUY IS APPROPRIATE FOR THE NEEDS OF YOUR AXOLOTL. IF UNSURE OF WHAT TO BUY, YOU CAN CONSULT YOUR LOCAL VETS OR THE KNOWN SHOP.

FOODS TO AVOID

BEEF HEART

BEEF HEARTS ARE FATTY AND OILY. FEEDING THIS CONTINUOUSLY TO YOUR AXOLOTL WILL RESULT IN HEALTH PROBLEMS WITH THE LIVER.

HUMAN FOODS AND OTHER PET FOODS

NEVER FEED YOUR AXOLOTL ANY HUMAN FOOD AND OTHER PET'S FOODS. THIS MIGHT CAUSE HEALTH PROBLEMS FOR YOUR AXOLOTL LATER ON.

INSECTS WITH TOUGH EXOSKELETON

AVOID GIVING ANY INSECTS OR CRUSTACEANS WITH TOUGH EXOSKELETONS TO YOUR AXOLOTL AS THEY ARE TOO HARD IN TEXTURE, AND YOUR AXOLOTL WILL NOT BE ABLE TO DIGEST THEM PROPERLY.

FISH FOODS

ALTHOUGH AXOLOTLS CAN EAT SOME FISH FOODS, YOU STILL HAVE TO CONSIDER THE TYPE OF FISH FOOD YOU ARE GIVING THEM AS WELL AS THE CONDITION OF YOUR PET. HERBIVOROUS TYPE OF FISH FOOD SHOULD BE AVOIDED.

FEEDER FISH

FEEDER FISH CAN CARRY PARASITES AND OTHER DISEASES THAT CAN BE TRANSFERRED TO YOUR AXOLOTL.

ALGAE WAFER

AXOLOTLS ARE CARNIVOROUS, SO FEEDING THEM ALGAE WAFERS IS NOT REALLY ADVISABLE.

BREAD

CONSUMING THIS CAN LEAD TO DIGESTIVE PROBLEMS FOR YOUR AXOLOTL.

PROCESSED MEATS

EVEN THOUGH AXOLOTLS ARE CONSIDERED CARNIVORES, FEEDING THEM ANY PROCESSED MEAT COULD LEAD TO A SERIOUS HEALTH PROBLEM. THEY ARE USUALLY LOADED WITH CHEMICALS AND PRESERVATIVES THAT ARE VERY HARMFUL TO YOUR PET.

YOU ALSO HAVE TO REMEMBER THAT APPETITE AND FOOD A VALUABLE INDICATORS OF YOUR AXOLOTL'S HEALTH. AND ALWAYS BUY YOUR AXOLOTL'S FOOD FROM A KNOWN SOURCE.

CARING FOR AXIES AS PETS

WHEN TAKING CARE OF ANY PETS, YOU HAVE TO BE KNOWLEDGEABLE AND FIRST DO EXTENSIVE RESEARCH TO GIVE YOUR PETS A GOOD ENVIRONMENT AND HEALTHY LIFESTYLE.

JUST LIKE TAKING CARE OF OTHER AQUATIC PETS, TAKING CARE OF AXOLOTLS REQUIRES GREAT CONSIDERATION. YOU MUST ENSURE THAT YOU WILL BE ABLE TO MEET THE FOLLOWING REQUIREMENTS.

AQUARIUM TANKS

THE RECOMMENDED TANKS TO HOUSE YOUR AXOLOTL IS AT LEAST 15-20 GALLONS. YOU ALSO HAVE TO MAKE SURE THAT THERE IS A SECURE LID FOR THESE AQUARIUM TANKS AS AXOLOTLS ARE KNOWN TO JUMP OUT OF THEIR ENCLOSURE.

YOU SHOULD ALWAYS PRIORITIZE THE LENGTH AND THE WIDTH OF THE TANK OVER THE HEIGHT AS YOUR AXOLOTL PET NEEDS PLENTY OF ROOM TO FREELY MOVE AND EXPLORE.

WATER REQUIREMENTS

THERE ARE A COUPLE OF REQUIREMENTS THAT NEED TO BE MET WHEN SETTING UP WATER FOR YOUR AXOLOTL'S AQUARIUM. ONE OF THEM IS THE TEMPERATURE OF THE WATER. AXOLOTLS ARE KNOWN TO THRIVE IN COLDER WATER TEMPERATURES SO YOU SHOULD ALWAYS KEEP THE TANK IN BETWEEN 15-18°C.

ASIDE FROM THE WATER TEMPERATURE, THE WATER'S PH LEVEL (BETWEEN 6.5 AND 8.0) SHOULD ALSO BE REGULARLY CHECKED AND MAINTAINED. YOU MUST ALSO MAKE SURE THAT THERE IS NO CHLORINE OR AMMONIA MIXED IN THE WATER THAT YOU WILL USE.

THERE ARE A COUPLE OF WAYS TO KEEP THE WATER IN YOUR AQUARIUM TANKS COOLER. YOU COULD USE AN AQUARIUM CHILLER, IT CAN BE A BIT PRICY BUT THIS TOOL IS VERY RELIABLE. YOU COULD ALSO USE AN AQUARIUM FAN AS WELL AS A MESH LID THAT ALLOWS FOR THE HEAT TO ESCAPE THE AQUARIUM TANK. SHOULD THERE BE AN EMERGENCY, YOU COULD USE DECHLORINATED ICE CUBES AS THIS WILL HELP COOL DOWN YOUR TANK.

YOU MUST ALSO REMEMBER THAT BEFORE PUTTING YOUR AXOLOTL IN THEIR TANK, THE WATER SHOULD UNDERGO A CYCLING PROCESS. IN THIS PROCESS, YOUR FILTER WILL TURN HARMFUL CHEMICALS LIKE AMMONIA INTO NITRITES AND THEN INTO NITRATE, A LESS POISONOUS CHEMICAL. (NITRATE SHOULD ALWAYS BE BETWEEN 5 AND 20 PPM)

WHEN CHOOSING A FILTER, MAKE SURE THAT IT HAS A SLOW FILTRATION RATE AS FAST FILTRATION CAN STRESS YOUR AXOLOTLS.

WATER CLEANING

WHEN REPLACING YOUR WATER, THERE ARE A COUPLE OF THINGS THAT YOU MUST REMEMBER. IF YOU USE A FILTER, YOU CAN CHANGE THE WATER EVERY WEEK AND TAKE NOTE TO REMOVE THE WASTE AT THE BOTTOM OF THE AQUARIUM. FOR TANKS WITHOUT FILTERS, YOU MUST CHANGE THE WATER EVERY OTHER DAY.

YOU MUST MAKE SURE TO ONLY REPLACE 20% OF THE WATER IN THE TANK AS DOING A FULL WATER CHANGE CAN DRASTICALLY CHANGE THE WATER CHEMICAL AND CAN CAUSE STRESS TO YOUR PET.

SUBSTRATE/GRAVEL

IF YOU ARE PLANNING ON PUTTING ANY SUBSTRATE OR GRAVEL ON YOUR AXOLOTL'S TANK, ALWAYS KEEP IN MIND THAT USING LOOSE SUBSTRATE AND SMALL PEBBLES CAN CAUSE HARM TO YOUR PET. YOUR AXOLOTL MIGHT ACCIDENTALLY INGEST THEM.

INSTEAD, YOU CAN USE SOFT AND FINE SANDS THAT ARE LESS THAN 1MM IN SIZE AS THIS ONLY POSES A LITTLE THREAT TO YOUR AXOLOTL. EVEN IF YOUR PET ACCIDENTALLY INGESTS THIS SAND, IT WILL ONLY PASS THROUGH THEM WITHOUT ANY PROBLEM.

HOWEVER, YOU MUST KEEP IN MIND THAT YOU MUST AVOID PUTTING BABY AXOLOTLS IN A TANK WITH ANY SUBSTRATE AS THEY ARE STILL VERY SMALL, YOU MUST WAIT UNTIL YOUR AXOLOTL IS AT LEAST 6 INCHES LONG.

PLANTS AND DECORATIONS

PUTTING PLANTS AND DECORATIONS ON YOUR AXOLOTL'S TANK IS IMPORTANT AS IT PROVIDES A COMFORTABLE ENVIRONMENT. PLANTS PROVIDE HIDING SPOTS FOR YOUR PETS. ALSO, HABITUALLY REARRANGING DECORATIONS CAN PROVIDE ENRICHMENT FOR YOUR PET AS THEY EXPLORE.

PLANTS CAN ALSO HELP WITH FILTERING THE NITRATE FROM YOUR WATER AND MAKE IT MORE HEALTHY FOR YOUR AXOLOTL.

HOWEVER, YOU MUST KEEP IN MIND THAT NOT ALL PLANTS ARE SUITABLE TO USE WHEN DECORATING YOUR AXOLOTL TANK. YOU MUST FIRST DO AN EXTENSIVE RESEARCH SO YOU CAN GIVE YOUR PET A HEALTHY AND SAFE ENVIRONMENT.

SOME SUITABLE PLANTS THAT YOU CAN USE ARE WATER WISTERIA, AMAZON SWORD, JAVA FERN, LUDWIGA, JAVA MOSS, BACOPA, AND ANUBIAS. YOU MUST ALSO TAKE NOTE THAT YOU CANNOT LIQUID FERTILIZERS AS AXOLOTLS MIGHT ABSORB IT.

REMEMBER TO CAREFULLY EXAMINE THE PLANTS THAT YOU WILL USE BEFORE PUTTING IT INSIDE THE TANK WITH YOUR PET.

IT IS BEST TO SEPARATE AND CAREFULLY OBSERVE THE PLANTS IN A DIFFERENT TANK FOR TWO WEEKS AS PEST SNAILS SOMETIMES SNEAK THEIR WAY INTO YOUR TANK.

LIGHTING

AXOLOTLS ARE KNOWN TO HAVE POOR VISION. THEY DO NOT HAVE EYELIDS THAT PROTECT THEIR EYES FROM ANY INTENSE LIGHTING. NOT ONLY CAN THIS INTENSE LIGHTING STRESS OUT YOUR PET BUT IT WILL ALSO HEAT THE WATER IN NO TIME WHICH WILL LEAD TO PROBLEMS, SO IT IS RECOMMENDED TO ONLY USE AMBIENT ROOM LIGHTING.

A GOOD SUGGESTION WOULD BE TO USE A PROGRAMMABLE LED LIGHT. YOU CAN USE IT TO GIVE ENOUGH LIGHT FOR YOUR PLANTS TO THRIVE WHILE YOUR AXOLOTL REMAINS COMFORTABLE.

WITH THIS, ALWAYS REMEMBER THAT YOU NEED TO KEEP A SCHEDULED MAINTENANCE AND CLEANING OF YOUR TANK. REMEMBER THAT ANY PET WILL THRIVE AND LIVE THEIR BEST LIFE IF GIVEN THE BEST TREATMENT AND CARE.

SIGNS OF STRESS IN AXOLOTLS

HERE ARE A COUPLE OF SIGNS YOU CAN OBSERVE IN YOUR PET IF IT IS STRESSED OUT FROM IT'S ENVIRONMENT:

DETERIORATION OF GILLS - THIS IS OFTEN CAUSED BY HIGH AMMONIA LEVEL IN WATER. THIS IS VERY DANGEROUS FOR YOUR PET.

CURLED GILLS - WHEN YOUR AXOLOTL'S GILLS ARE CURLED OUTWARDS TOWARDS YOUR AXIE'S FACE, THIS MEANS THAT YOUR PET IS STRESSED OUT AND UNHAPPY.

APPETITE LOSS - THIS IS THE MOST COMMON SIGN OF STRESS IN AXOLOTLS, ONE OF THE CAUSE OF THIS IS THE WATER TEMPERATURE.

VERY ACTIVE AXOLOTL - WHEN YOUR AXOLOTL IS SWIMMING FRANTICALLY, IT COMMONLY INDICATES THAT YOUR PET IS IN PAIN. OR SOMETHING IS CAUSING IT PAIN.

FREQUENT AIR GULPS - THIS IS A SIGN OF HAVING A WARM WATER. IF YOU NOTICE THAT YOUR AXOLOTL SWIM TO THE SURFACE TO GET SOME AIR, THEN QUICKLY CHECK THE WATER TEMPERATURE.

FLOATING IN WATER - THIS COULD BE A SIGN OF AN AIR ENTERING ITS GASTRIC SYSTEM.

HEALTH ISSUES IN AXOLOTL

WOUNDS - WOUNDS LIKE CUTS, BITES OR MISSING LIMBS IS VERY COMMON IN AXOLOTLS. THERE'S NO NEED TO WORRY AS THEY HAVE REGENERATIVE ABILITY. HOWEVER, HEALING WILL STILL DEPEND OF CERTAIN FACTORS LIKE SEVERITY OF THE WOUND, YOUR AXOLOTL'S AGE, AS WELL AS THEIR ENVIRONMENT.

FUNGUS - THIS IS VERY COMMON IF YOU DO NOT PROPERLY CLEAN AND MAINTAIN YOUR AQUARIUM TANKS. ALTHOUGH THIS PROBLEM IS VERY EASY TO DEAL WITH, IT COULD STILL BRING DANGER TO YOUR PET.

CHEMICAL BURN - THIS ONE IS ONE OF THE VERY PAINFUL CONDITION THAT CAN HAPPEN TO YOUR PET. AXOLOTL'S SKIN WITH CHEMICAL BURN WILL APPEAR RED. IT IS IMPORTANT TO TAKE QUICK ACTION.

PARASITIC INFECTION - CAN BE CAUSED BY POOR WATER QUALITY OR LIVE FOODS. MAKE SURE TO CONSULT YOUR VET TO KNOW THE RIGHT TREATMENT FOR YOUR AXOLOTL.

BACTERIAL INFECTION - THERE ARE DIFFERENT TYPES OF BACTERIAL INFECTION. IN ORDER TO AVOID THIS, MAKE SURE TO PROPERLY CLEAN YOUR TANK AND STRICTLY FOLLOW THE GUIDELINES IN RAISING AXOLOTLS.

CONSERVATION & THREATS TO AXIES

IN THE WILD, AXOLOTLS NUMBER IS IN GREAT DECLINE. IT WAS ESTIMATED THAT AROUND 50 TO 1,000 AXOLOTLS ARE LEFT LIVING IN THE WILD. THERE ARE A LOT OF FACTORS THAT THREATEN AN AXOLOTL'S POPULATION.

ONE OF THEM IS A HUGE INCREASE IN THE SPECIES OF INVASIVE FISH THAT ARE NOT NATIVE TO XOCHIMILCO LAKE. SOME OF THE INVASIVE FISH SPECIES THAT WERE INTRODUCED TO THE WATERWAYS ARE TILAPIA AND CARP. THESE INVASIVE FISHES REPRODUCE AT A HIGH SPEED AND CAN TIP OFF THE BALANCE OF THE LAKE'S POPULATION.

NOT ONLY THAT, THESE INVASIVE FISH SPECIES COMPETE WITH THE AXOLOTLS FOR FOOD, WHICH IN TURN THREATEN THE SURVIVAL OF THE AXOLOTLS WITH SCARCITY OF AVAILABLE RESOURCES FOR THEM TO EAT. BUT THEY ALSO HUNT AXOLOTLS FOR FOOD. THESE INVASIVE FISHES ARE A GREAT THREAT, ESPECIALLY TO THE AXOLOTLS THAT JUST NEWLY HATCHED.

IT IS KNOWN THAT AXOLOTLS NEED AQUATIC PLANTS TO LAY THEIR EGGS ON AND DEEP WATERS TO HELP THEM THRIVE, BUT WITH THE URBANIZATION AROUND THEIR NATIVE LAKE, THEIR NATURAL HABITAT HAS BEEN SHRINKING GREATLY.

ANOTHER FACTOR WHY URBANIZATION CAUSES THE DECLINE OF AXOLOTL SPECIES IS THE POLLUTION THAT IT BRINGS. WITH PEOPLE INCREASING IN NUMBERS AROUND THE AXOLOTL'S NATURAL HABITAT, IT IS NOT A SURPRISE THAT THE WATER IN THE LAKE IS SLOWLY GETTING POLLUTED, POISONING ALL THE SPECIES LIVING IN IT, INCLUDING THE AXOLOTLS.

THIS IS THE REASON THAT AXOLOTL'S LIFESPAN LIVING IN THE WILD ONLY ADDS UP TO ABOUT FIVE TO SIX YEARS.

AS OF TODAY, THERE ARE AN ESTIMATED OF AROUND 1,000 AXOLOTLS IN THE WILD. YOU CAN HELP WITH THE CONSERVATION OF THIS SPECIES BY DOING YOUR BEST NOT TO POLLUTE THE WATER SOURCES AS WELL AS BY HELPING OTHERS RAISE AWARENESS ABOUT THESE ADOBRALE AXOLOTLS.

BREEDING & GENETICS

AXOLOTL'S BREEDING EVENT CAN HAPPEN UP TO THREE TIMES DEPENDING ON WHETHER THEY ARE LIVING IN THE WILD OR IN CAPTIVITY. CONSISTENT WITH THEIR NATURE OF BEING ADORABLE, AXOLOTL'S ACT OF COURTING IS SIMPLY THE SAME.

THIS RITUAL IS SIMILAR TO A DANCE WHERE THE MALE AXOLOTL SHAKES HIS TAIL AND LOWER BODY. THE FEMALE AXOLOTL RESPONDS BY NUDGING THE DANCER IN FRONT OF HER USING HER SNOUT.

THE MALE AXOLOTL WILL THEN PUT WHAT THEY CALL "SPERMATOPHORES" ON THE LAKE FLOOR WHILE THE FEMALE WILL PICK THESE UP AND HELP WITH THE FERTILIZATION OF EGGS THAT WILL THEN TURN INTO LARVAE. THE FEMALE AXOLOTL WILL LAY THESE EGGS ON PLANTS AND ROCKS. THERE'S ANOTHER TWO WEEKS FOR THEM TO HATCH.

DID YOU KNOW THAT, AS OF RIGHT NOW, THERE ARE OVER 20 DIFFERENT KNOWN COLORS AND MORPHS OF AXOLOTL? THIS IS ALL THANKS TO THE THREE COLOR PIGMENT CHROMATOPHORES, MELANOPHORES, XANTHOPHORES, AND IRIDOPHORES, WHICH ARE FOUND ON THEIR SKIN AND HELP DETERMINE THE FINAL COLOR OF AN AXOLOTL.

THERE ARE A COUPLE OF GENETIC TRAITS ALREADY DISCOVERED, LIKE AXANTHIC (MORE PURPLE/GRAY COLORATION) AND ALBINISM (WHITE COLORATION WITH PINK EYES AND GILLS).

THE NEWEST GENETIC TRAIT OF AN AXOLOTL THAT WAS DISCOVERED WAS CALLED HYPOMELANOID. THIS RARE GENETIC TRAIT IS CHARACTERIZED BY HAVING GENES THAT CAN EXPRESS MELANISM BUT IT WOULD NOT APPEAR ON THEIR BODY.

THE FUTURE OF AXOLOTLS

TODAY, AXOLOTL'S EXISTENCE ARE AT THE RISK OF EXTINCTION. THEY ARE ALREADY CLASSIFIED AS ENDANGERED AS ONLY A FEW OF THEM ARE CURRENTLY LIVING IN THE WILD, WHILE MOST NUMBERS ARE FOUND IN PETSHOPS.

AXIES ARE KNOWN FOR THEIR MAGNIFICENT REGENERATING ABILITIES. HOWEVER, WITH THE DECLINE OF THEIR NUMBERS, SCIENTISTS ARE CONCERNED AS THIS WOULD HINDER THE ADVANCEMENT OF MEDICINAL SCIENTIFIC DISCOVERIES AND BREAKTHROUGHS.

THIS IS ONE OF THE REASONS THAT WE MUST DO EVERYTHING WE CAN TO CONSERVE AND PROTECT AXOLOTLS. THE PRESERVATION OF AXOLOTLS ARE ENTIRELY UP TO US.

THE FUTURE OF THE AXOLOTL SPECIES SEEMS BLEAK. ANOTHER FACTOR THAT CAN AFFECT THEIR FUTURE IS THE THREAT OF CLIMATE CHANGE. EXTREME DROUGHT THREATENS THE LOSS OF THEIR HABITAT. WHEN THAT HAPPENS, AXOLOTLS HAVE NO CHOICE BUT TO EVOLVE TO SURVIVE.

DUE TO WATER CONTAMINATION IN THE FUTURE, AXOLOTLS ARE SPECULATED TO EVOLVE FROM BEING A WATER ANIMAL TO LAND ANIMALS. THEY WILL STILL BE ABLE TO SWIM AND CATCH THEIR PREY.

WINDSTORMS WILL FREQUENTLY HAPPEN SO AXOLOTLS WOULD NEED TO GROW ARMS SO THAT THEY COULD BURROW IN THE SAND FOR SAFETY. ASIDE FROM BEING A LAND ANIMAL, AXOLOTL WILL HAVE FINS LIKE OTHER FISHES AND THEY MIGHT EVEN BE ABLE TO SWIM LIKE FLYING FISHES.

THIS FUTURE SEEMED FARFETCHED BUT WITH THE RATE OF HOW EVERYTHING IS GOING NOW, IT DOESN'T SEEM SO IMPOSSIBLE. SO WE MUST DO OUR PART IN SAVING AND CONSERVING THE AXOLOTL SPECIES.

AXOLOTL QUIZ

WHERE DO AXOLOTLS LIVE?

A. LAND
B. WATER
C. CAVES
D. TREES

WHERE DO AXOLOTLS ORIGINALLY FOUND?

A. MURKY FRESH WATER LAKES AND CANALS IN XOCHIMILCO.
B. VENICE GRAND CANAL
C. NILE RIVER
D. DESSERT

WHAT DO YOU CALL AXOLOTL'S SPECIAL ABILITY THAT CAN HELP REGROW THEIR INJURED LIMBS?

A. CAMOUFLAGE
B. HIBERNATION
C. LASER EYES
D. REGENERATION

HOW MANY TEETH DOES AN AXOLOTL HAVE?

A. ZERO
B. FIVE
C. TEN
D. THREE

WHAT IS THE SCIENTIFIC NAME OF AXOLOTL?

A. AMBYSTOMA MEXICANUM
B. FELIS CATUS
C. SELACHIMORPHA
D. PANTHERA LEO

WHICH OF THE FOLLOWING ARE A GOOD TANK MATE FOR YOUR AXOLOTL?

A. TILAPIA
B. SHRIMPS
C. GUPPIES
D. PANTHERA LEO

TRUE OR FALSE: AXOLOTLS PREFER TO LIVE IN WARM WATER.

A. TRUE
B. FALSE

WHICH OF THE FOLLOWING ARE THE DIFFERENT COLORS OF AXOLOTL?

A. ALBINISM (WHITE COLORATION WITH PINK EYES OR GILLS)
B. AXANTHIC (MORE PURPLE/GRAY IN COLORATION)
C. HYPOMELANOID
D. ALL OF THE ABOVE

WHICH OF THE FOLLOWING IS NOT A SUITABLE PLANT TO USE IN YOUR AXOLOTL'S TANK?

A. JAVA MOSS
B. SALVINIA
C. BACOPA
D. JAVA FERN

AXOLOTLS ARE KNOWN AS:

A. CARNIVORE
B. HERBIVORE
C. OMNIVORE
D. AVIVORE

L	E	A	X	A	N	T	H	I	C	P	G	G	E
E	A	T	A	I	T	M	P	R	L	T	L	C	X
A	A	I	P	N	I	A	A	M	A	A	C	S	H
X	A	T	H	K	L	X	X	E	X	X	E	E	N
I	A	A	B	T	A	C	O	X	S	E	T	I	A
E	I	N	N	L	P	T	E	I	I	G	Z	P	I
S	A	A	E	T	I	A	A	C	I	P	A	P	B
E	E	X	V	P	A	L	L	O	X	A	H	U	I
L	L	T	O	N	A	A	E	R	E	I	N	G	H
A	X	A	S	L	C	K	A	A	A	N	A	I	P
R	L	A	E	O	O	E	P	A	O	H	A	O	M
V	X	A	O	A	C	T	H	A	E	P	I	I	A
A	E	A	N	R	A	I	L	A	I	A	T	H	O
E	T	A	R	E	N	E	G	E	R	D	N	A	P

AXOLOTL **REGENERATE** **AMPHIBIAN** **TILAPIA**
AXANTHIC **GUPPIES** **AZTEC** **LARVAE**
AXIES **DAPHNIA** **LAKE** **MEXICO**

FAQ'S

WHAT IS A MORPHED AXOLOTL?

MORPHING IS THE INSTANCE WHERE AXOLOTLS CHANGES ITS FORM. THIS IS USUALLY DUE TO CHANGES IN THEIR ENVIRONMENT. WHEN THIS HAPPEN, YOU MUST MAKE SURE TO CLOSELY OBSERVE YOUR PET FOR ANY CHANGES THAT COULD BE HARMFUL TO THEM.

CAN AXOLOTLS SURVIVE IN PONDS?

THIS WILL ACTUALLY DEPEND ON THE OVERALL WEATHER AND TEMPERATURE OF YOUR LOCATION. AS LONG AS THE WATER TEMPERATURE DOES NOT EXCEED 15-18°C ALL YEAR ROUND.

WHAT TO DO IF MY AXOLOTL ACCIDENTALLY SWALLOWED GRAVEL?

AXOLOTLS WILL USUALLY PASS GRAVELS WITHOUT ANY PROBLEM. HOWEVER, THERE ARE INSTANCES THAT IT CAN CAUSE BLOCKAGE. PUT YOUR AXOLOTL IN A CLEAR BOTTOM TANK AND CONTINUOUSLY OBSERVE IT FOR TWO WEEKS.

WHAT DO I DO IF MY AXOLOTL STOP EATING?

CHECK THE WATER'S TEMPERATURE, THIS USUALLY HAPPEN WHEN THE TEMPERATURE IS TOO HIGH AND CAUSES DISCOMFORT TO YOUR PET. TRY TO COOL DOWN THE WATER FOR ABOUT 5-10°C AND OBSERVE FOR 10-14 DAYS BEFORE YOU SLOWLY WARM IT UP.

HOW TO IDENTIFY MY AXOLOTL'S GENDER?

YOU WILL NEED TO WAIT FOR 18 MONTHS BEFORE YOU CAN IDENTIFY YOUR AXOLOTL'S GENDER. THE MALE AXOLOTL HAS A SLIMMER BODY AND LONGER TAIL, THEIR SWOLLEN REPRODUCTIVE GLANDS AROUND THEIR CLOACA IS ALSO NOTICEABLE. WHILE THE FEMALE AXOLOTL HAVE SMALLER CLOACA AND ROUNDER BODIES.

IS IT OKAY TO PICK UP AND HOLD MY AXOLOTL?

AXIES DOESN'T REALLY LIKE TO BE HELD OFTEN, THIS STRESSES THEM OUT. HOWEVER, IF YOU DO TO TOUCH THEM WHEN TRANSFERRING TO ANOTHER TANK, MAKE SURE YOU PROPERLY WASHED YOUR HANDS TO REMOVE CHEMICALS LIKE LOTIONS OR HAND SANITIZER. REMEMBER TO APPROACH THEM GENTLY AND BE VERY CAREFUL.

METAMORPHOSIS - THE CHANGE THAT ANIMALS GO THROUGH DURING THEIR GROWTH CYCLE.

NEOTENIC - THIS IS WHEN AN ANIMAL ENTERS THEIR ADULT PHASE BUT STILL RETAINS THEIR JUVENILE FORM.

NITRATE - THIS IS A CHEMICAL THAT IS USEFUL IN PLANT GROWTH.

NITRITE - THIS IS A POISONOUS COMPOUND THAT IS TRANSFORMED FROM AMMONIA.

PARASITE - THIS IS AN ORGANISM THAT LIVES INSIDE ANOTHER ORGANISM.

PESTICIDE - THIS IS A SUBSTANCE THAT IS USE TO KILL PESTS ON PLANTS.

PREDATOR - ANY ANIMAL THAT HUNTS OTHER ANIMALS FOR FOOD.

PROTEIN - THIS IS AN IMPORTANT NUTRIENT THAT IS NEEDED FOR THE BODY TO FUNCTION.

REGENERATIVE - THE PROCESS OF GENERATING NEW LIMBS TO REPLACE ANY BODY PARTS.

SUBSTRATE - A SURFACE WHERE AN ORGANISM LIVES AND GROWS.

URBANIZATION - THIS REFERS TO THE INCREASE OF POPULATION IN CITIES FROM FARMS AREAS.

WINDSTORM - A STRONG WIND THAT CAUSES LIGHT DAMAGE TO TREES AND BUILDINGS.

XOCHIMILCO - IS A CANAL THAT IS LOCATED IN MEXICO WHERE AXOLOTLS ARE FOUND.

GLOSSARY

AMMONIA - THIS CHEMICAL CAUSES A DIRECT TOXIC EFFECTS IN AQUATIC LIFE.

AMPHIBIAN - ANIMALS THAT CAN LIVE BOTH ON LAND AND IN WATER.

ANTIBIOTIC - A MEDICINE THAT HELPS FIGHT BACTERIAL INFECTION.

CARNIVORE - ANY ANIMAL THAT EATS MEAT.

CLOACA - A CHAMBER AT THE END OF THE DIGESTIVE TRACT IN AMPHIBIANS WHERE THE GENITAL, INTESTINAL, AND URINARY TRACTS OPEN.

CRUSTACEANS - ANIMALS THAT HAS A HARD COVERING OR EXOSKELETON

AND TWO PAIRS OF ANTENNAS.

DECHLORINATED - A WATER THAT IS REMOVED OF ANY CHLORINE.

DETERIORATION - THIS PROCESS THAT DESCRIBE SOMETHING BECOMING PROGRESSIVELY WORSE.

FUNGUS - ORGANISM THAT FEEDS ON DEAD MATERIAL.

GASTRIC SYSTEM - DIGESTIVE SYSTEM

GILLS - PART OF BODY OF AQUATIC CREATURES THAT HELP THEM BREATHE UNDERWATER.

HABITAT - THE HOME OF ANIMAL OR PLANTS.

LARVAE - AN ANIMAL THAT HATCHES FROM EGG.

ACTIVITY ANSWERS

WHERE DO AXOLOTLS LIVE?

A. LAND
B. WATER
C. CAVES
D. TREES

WHERE DO AXOLOTLS ORIGINALLY FOUND?

A. MURKY FRESH WATER LAKES AND CANALS IN XOCHIMILCO.
B. VENICE GRAND CANAL
C. NILE RIVER
D. DESSERT

WHAT DO YOU CALL AXOLOTL'S SPECIAL ABILITY THAT CAN HELP REGROW THEIR INJURED LIMBS?

A. CAMOUFLAGE
B. HIBERNATION
C. LASER EYES
D. REGENERATION

HOW MANY TEETH DOES AN AXOLOTL HAVE?

A. ZERO

B. FIVE

C. TEN

D. THREE

WHAT IS THE SCIENTIFIC NAME OF AXOLOTL?

A. AMBYSTOMA MEXICANUM

B. FELIS CATUS

C. SELACHIMORPHA

D. PANTHERA LEO

WHICH OF THE FOLLOWING ARE A GOOD TANK MATE FOR YOUR AXOLOTL?

A. TILAPIA

B. SHRIMPS

C. GUPPIES

D. PANTHERA LEO

TRUE OR FALSE: AXOLOTLS PREFER TO LIVE IN WARM WATER.

A. TRUE

B. FALSE - AXIES PREFER TO LIVE IN COOL WATERS

WHICH OF THE FOLLOWING ARE THE DIFFERENT COLORS OF AXOLOTL?

A. ALBINISM (WHITE COLORATION WITH PINK EYES OR GILLS)
B. AXANTHIC (MORE PURPLE/GRAY IN COLORATION)
C. HYPOMELANOID
D. ALL OF THE ABOVE

WHICH OF THE FOLLOWING IS NOT A SUITABLE PLANT TO USE IN YOUR AXOLOTL'S TANK?

A. JAVA MOSS
B. SALVINIA
C. BACOPA
D. JAVA FERN

AXOLOTLS ARE KNOWN AS:

A. CARNIVORE
B. HERBIVORE
C. OMNIVORE
D. AVIVORE

L	E	A	X	A	N	T	H	I	C	P	G	G	E
E	A	T	A	I	T	M	P	R	L	T	L	C	X
A	A	I	P	N	I	A	A	M	A	A	C	S	H
X	A	T	H	K	L	X	X	E	X	X	E	E	N
I	A	A	B	T	A	C	O	X	S	E	T	I	A
E	I	N	N	L	P	T	E	I	I	G	Z	P	I
S	A	A	E	T	I	A	A	C	I	P	A	P	B
E	E	X	V	P	A	L	L	O	X	A	H	U	I
L	L	T	O	N	A	A	E	R	E	I	N	G	H
A	X	A	S	L	C	K	A	A	A	N	A	I	P
R	L	A	E	O	O	E	P	A	O	H	A	O	M
V	X	A	O	A	C	T	H	A	E	P	I	I	A
A	E	A	N	R	A	I	L	A	I	A	T	H	O
E	T	A	R	E	N	E	G	E	R	D	N	A	P

www.ingramcontent.com/pod-product-compliance
Ingram Content Group UK Ltd.
Pitfield, Milton Keynes, MK11 3LW, UK
UKHW051342030625
6213UKWH00029B/422

9 781915 363923